ENGAGEMENT

ENGAGEMENT

Çiler İlhan

Translated from the Turkish
by

KENNETH DAKAN

istrosbooks

Translated from the Turkish
by
KENNETH DAKAN

ENGAGEMENT

To the precious children of Our Village

EAU DE COLOGNE

Maral had forgotten all about the eau de cologne even though her mother had reminded her two days previously: 'You can't hold out a bottle of warm cologne for guests. It's bought beforehand, kept in the fridge and splashed cold onto cupped palms.' What a bad start to the day! Surely no good will come of it.

And so, it fell on Halil to get the scent, since Maral and her favorite aunt, never-married Nasibe (in this place, an unmarried woman is an old maid, a spinster or stuck-at-home–so let us say, instead, that Maral and her favorite aunt, the Spinster Nasibe) were supposed to go door-to-door to invite guests over for the evening. Maral had her work cut out for her. You see, Nasibe only has one good arm; the left one was stunted and useless. The village had more than its fair share of crazies and cripples. City people came once to do research: 'If you people keep marrying each other,' a woman in thick-rimmed glasses said, 'nothing will ever change.'

It was a beautiful morning. In the month of May. What can turn green, has. The people down on the plains call those living here *cayı*, meaning 'mountain people'. But there are no mountains. There are rolling hills, and at their feet greenery blossoming in spring sunshine. Green, green, yellow. Yellow, yellow, flatness. Flat, flat, hill. So goes the landscape in these parts, where sheep far outnumber fields. Such a perfect day, were it not for the sandstorm. Or, actually, the sandstorm might have swept in near sundown.

I'll wear my new shoes now so they're broken in by the evening.

That is what Halil was thinking.

But the soles were leather. And bound to slip.

CHUNKY

They were not his first pair of leather shoes, of course. Few households were forced to scrape by in this village; most had plenty. This was true of his father Hasan and his mother Gülüm. True too of his youngest aunt, Nasibe, and his elder aunts, Hatice and Rahime. Of his Uncle Ömer, too. And from this abundance would come all the trouble.

But it was Chunky that caused the first tumble.

Halil loved morning milk fresh from the cow, always had done. They say a prize cock crows in the egg; well, you could still cradle him in two hands when he started favoring cow's milk over his mother's. But Chunky grew uneasy that day when he reached for her udder from behind. She never did that, but animal instinct might have told her that today was no ordinary day. She threw her bulk into a kick, as if they were coming to cut her throat. True to her name, Chunky was the fattest cow around.

Halil lost his balance and banged his head hard, leaving him dazed. Chunky was confused too. As Halil moaned and groaned flat on his back, she went up and licked him.

What a bother on this of all days! Who had time to take Halil to a clinic in town when everybody was already up to their ears in work? 'Ah, Halil, you're every bit as clumsy as your mother says!'

LEYLA

Her hair was like her name. Dark as the night. Cloaking her to the waist. Bilal had been smitten by this hair while still a boy. This he told to Leyla many years later. When she reached the age of twenty, and continued to reject all her matches–including the son of an uncle a few weeks previously–her father Cemal had decided in anger to give her in marriage to Tahsin, a relative from town, so she would not end up a 'stuck-at-home'. The second he heard, Bilal jumped into his Renault and gulped down seventy kilometres of road quick as a pill. In this village, men know to stay away when the man of the house is gone.

Bilal, a blood relation on his mother's side, stepped right up and knocked on the front door. It was opened by Leyla's mother, Fatma, she too, with hair like the night. When she saw Bilal standing there, so pale, she understood immediately. Fatma was such a sensitive soul. She really was. When he stammered something about having business in the village and his last-minute decision to drop by, she believed him, or so she made him believe.

'Come sit for a bit and I'll make you coffee,' she said, waving him in.

Bilal took his towering frame inside. In the village, his cousin clumsy Halil was called 'Tall Halil,' for he had been lanky as a boy, though often sickly and bed-ridden. Back then, all the thrashings in the world could not persuade him to clean his supper plate. But unlike Halil, Bilal was a roly-poly boy, with a good appetite. Now the cousins had both grown into poplars.

Here, they call the biggest room in the house the *divanhane*. Leyla's father was once the village headman, meaning many visitors streamed in and out of this house, and still did. These homes are spacious compared to city apartments whose bedrooms are no bigger than chickpeas and whose sitting rooms are broad beans at best. Bilal picked his way across the precious carpets and sat down on one of the floor cushions lining the walls. His back comfortably up against yellow, green and purple pillows shrouded in white lace, he brought his fingers to the end of his mustache and twisted, fidgeting away the minutes. It was the scant mustache of a man of twenty-two, and pristine. The mad dash here was all well and good, but what now? His heart beat something terrible for Leyla. He couldn't say anything about this, though, not to the women of the house. What a mistake! Pulling himself together, he decided he would head back as soon as the usual small talk had petered out. As he sprawled against the pillows, hands on his knees, his eyes landed on a skillfully embroidered Shahmaran motif: straight into the eyes of this wise half-woman/half-snake who legend told had been killed so that Man could gain curative powers. Was she trying to tell him something?

Bilal squirmed and sighed as Fatma prepared coffee in a kitchen whose supply of pots and pans could easily have cooked up a feast for hundreds. She called her eldest daughter, Leyla, to her side.

'Here, take this coffee to Bilal,' she instructed. 'And if you've got something to say, girl, say it now.'

Should Fatma have known better than to bring those two lovebirds together? Perhaps. But then again, there is no getting around fate.

ROAD

Halil walked past the village houses, some nicely plastered and others half-naked; most built of hollow clay blocks and a few made of sun-dried brick. They were all one or two stories tall, with flat terrace roofs. The men were either on guard or asleep, out with the herds or tending the fields. The women were rocking babies or washing windows, kneading dough for *sembusek* or crushing tomatoes for paste. Children too young for school were out in the streets barefoot playing ride-the-horse, military police games, hide-and-go-seek, jump rope, five stones and dodgeball. But for the dark clouds gathering overhead, it was a perfectly ordinary day. Or perhaps it was closer to evening when the clouds came.

With the boundless energy of a sixteen-year-old and no thought for his splitting headache, Halil scurried along in his leather-soled shoes and a white short-sleeved shirt. The grocer's shop in the square was open early, as always, but the apprentice was manning the till, which meant that the owner, Fatty Bekir, must have been snoring away still in his bed. There was not a single bottle of cologne to be had, yet alone ten. As luck would have it. Nobody would see this as Halil's bad luck, though. They would say that Fatma and Cemal neglected to offer the annual sacrifice at Sheykh Shrine. That they failed to distribute the obligatory alms to the poor. That they not only skipped a few of their five-times-a-day prayers, but they also pleaded high blood pressure and soaring sugar levels so that, long before sundown, they could gobble bread and cheese behind closed curtains during Ramadan. Some would say that is what caused their terrible misfortune. When the boss is away, the tongues of the minions wag. Others would point to the long-running trout farm dispute between the family in Our Village and the family in Other Village. 'That's what caused the catastrophe,' they would say.

What complicated matters even more was that everyone was related, both in Our Village and in Other Village; furthermore, everyone in Our Village had blood ties to everyone in Other Village. The five fingers of the same hand are indeed similar, but is it fair to say that they are all the same? The gunmen, every last one of them, were from Other Village, just six or seven kilometres down the road. All of them were relatives of Halil and Leyla. The beetle bores from within the tree. And it is a fact that Sultan was both the mother of the ringleader and Leyla's eldest aunt.

Yes, the ringleader was Osman. And his mother was Sultan, the unluckiest of seven siblings. For she, mother of hind-leg-of-the-devil Osman, was also Halil's eldest aunt, and the very same Sultan who had shielded her eight children from a masked squad many years previously, during a late night raid. The Sultan, mother of my-way-or-the-highway Osman, who was struck by the squad leader's bullet. The Sultan, mother of suck-a-man-dry Osman, who was blamed when her husband just up and disappeared one day; the Sultan whose house was muddied by military boots once a week; the Sultan whose oldest son was killed by a guerrilla during military service. Turn over any stone and there was Osman's mother, Sultan, she who never lived up to her birth name and never knew a moment of luxury; she who crumpled into a blood-red rag in front of her children with a bullet in her chest, dead. And what did young Osman do? What could he do? His big brother was dead and his father was long-gone. He was the head of the house now. If counted one by one, his years on this earth came to fifteen, years that squeezed him dry and left him hard. Well, what Osman did was collect his seven orphaned siblings and move to Other Village. That was the day that Osman–calculating Osman, ringleader Osman, sheik Osman–picked up a taste for tobacco. All while on the move.

HALİL

Halil saw that there was no cologne to be had in Our Village, so where was the nearest place to get some? In Other Village, where Osman lived. It was six or seven kilometres away. The walk would take about an hour.

It is true that Halil's mother saw him as a clumsy fool, but he must have had a capable side, too, for how else would he have been one of only three people to give the shroud the slip on that black night? The rest would be buried in the village graveyard he was nearing on his journey that day. Halil did not like graveyards one bit, but this one was situated right at the village entrance and he had no choice but to pass it. This place was full of memories hazy and razor-sharp. When he fell into a fever as a boy of four, his parents had decided to take him there. To Sheykh Shrine. You know, that freshly entombed sheykh who rose to his feet as though to perform the standing part of his *namaz* prayers. The sheykh who made the poor, rich; who made the blind, see and made the sick, well. That sheykh. This was the nineties, an era when the state blacklisted the entire region and security checkpoints controlled access to every town.

There were no health services anywhere near the village and travel risked trouble, so his mother Gülüm and father Hasan bundled their boy in their arms and made their way to the edge of the village, to Sheykh Shrine. So fiery with fever was his little forehead that if unleashed it could have scorched the mountains and plains. As they passed the cemetery, ghosts were visible above the tombstones; disembodied heads, floating and flitting a few meters above the white slabs. Yet they seemed cheerful, those heads, and a few of them had winked and smiled at Halil. But he wet himself anyway. Putting it down to fever, his mother did not get cross with him at the time, and there was no whack with a stick. But his father let loose a terrible curse. How could a child of his, a little man no less, be pissing his pants at this age?

They stayed at the shrine for three nights, with Halil desert-hot the whole while. 'We take the boy to a hospital or you see me dead,' is what burst from Gülüm as she threw herself at her husband's feet. It worked. Hasan lay Halil in the back of the car, and off they drove to Town. When they got there the hospital's power was out. The doctor in the emergency ward said they should take Hasan to the city. Upper City or Lower City? Upper City was better equipped, but Lower City was closer. So off they went to Lower City. It took the self-sacrificing doctors two days to save Halil, but with the warning that his delayed treatment could lead to permanent damage, the extent of which would be clear only when he was older. Well, nobody's perfect.

That is why Halil gets uneasy skirting graveyards. What kind of person remembers seeing ghosts at age four? Someone like Halil, whose memory is always a bit of a muddle, not unlike the local *tırşık* served with meat and rice: a bit of eggplant, a bit of potato, a few peas, a bit of tomato, some green pepper, some zucchini, and thyme, onion, garlic...

He passed by the graveyard trembling that day. A few kilometres later, he came across another one.

'There's no escaping death,' he muttered, 'graveyards everywhere you go.'

Mouthing every prayer he knew, he scurried past the small burial ground across from the well-known tomb. Next to the entrance to the main cemetery, his eye landed on a corrugated metal awning supported by a concrete wall and iron posts, a sales point for sacrificial animals fenced in on three sides. Some brought their own offerings and others bought from this strange stall with a sign that read 'Animal Sell Place'. Someone who spoke Turkish as a second language had prepared the sign, or so Halil assumed, because Turkish was taught in these parts rather than learned. It was beaten into you at school, during military service or in prison. He was proud of his own Turkish, though, and received compliments whenever he came across visitors whose first language it was. He liked his own neglected Kurdish tongue well enough, too, having learned it at his mother's knee, but Turkish seemed more refined, somehow. At the sight and sound of the lambs and sheep he went all funny inside, again. Eating them was fine but seeing them like this was not. Did they know they were going to die? People didn't know. If they did, they wouldn't go on living.

It was at that point that he realized he was thirsty. He hadn't brought any water and it was a hot day. The sun was saying, *here I am*, from somewhere below the hilltop horizon. Halil decided to get a bottle of water from a shop inside. He stepped through the main cemetery gate and was asked to pay for entrance. When his protestations fell on deaf ears, he reached into his pocket. He was about to dig in his heels when it occurred to him that the place wouldn't be so green and clean if everyone claimed to be from the village and tried to get in for free, and he felt immediately sorry for being such an idiot. He was also sorry he had gone inside in the first place. This was a cemetery, after all! Those who come into this world return from whence they came; there is no escape. With quick steps he skirted the graves to his right. He considered pausing to recite a Fatiha for the souls of the dead but his fear got the better of him.

Halil went on to the aptly named We've Got It All Mall and entered through the first door of a series of three or four elongated shops stocking everything from sweets to toys, from trays to shalwar, from souvenirs to shoes. Half of the icy bottle of water he drank on the spot. As always, the place was heaving. An army of supplicants had placed their shoes on the shelves at the entrance to the Sheykh's mausoleum and were fidgeting in stocking feet as they shuffled in line. It was spacious inside. The Sheykh was interred in the middle of the main room, while the tombs of some of his followers were ringed around or housed in smaller adjoining rooms. But it was the Sheykh's wooden sarcophagus topped with a wrapping of turban cloth that drew the crowds. Men and women both would sit there for hours, stretch out on the floor or leave a sick friend or relative behind. It was said that after only a few hours people with mental illnesses, in particular, would go home cured; women whose doctors said they could never have children would, after a visit to this tomb, first dream of becoming a mother and then conceive soon afterwards. The inside of the mausoleum glowed with a dim green light day and night. But the stone walls were no defense against the heat, so all year round a white stand fan was stationed next to a yellow vacuum cleaner to the right of the arched doorway of the smallest of the three rooms.

Out in the open, too, it was so crowded that if you tossed a needle into the air, it would not hit the ground. Nobody tires of praying. Or of hoping. The lucky ones found a spot under a rough roof of vines, or against a wall; those unable to find shade had to settle for a patch of grass. Bread and cheese were placed on tablecloths and tea was made on portable gas canisters. Children played, women chatted, and men smoked and looked around with one leg tucked underneath them and the other bent at the knee, foot firmly planted on the ground. It was a spot for prayer, for livestock sales, for ritual offerings, for recreation, for shopping, for vendors... The main entrance opened onto a long corridor lined by stalls heaped high with tomatoes, peppers, grapes, lentils, pickles... There were no touts here, though, in this hushed holy place. Goods were sold in silence.

The pitiful bleats of a sheep shook Halil out of his thoughts. Had his mother seen him at that moment, she would have scolded him for his constant daydreaming. The sheep baa-ed and baa-ed as its new owner dragged it along by a rope round the neck. Who knew what the owner was wishing for? What he was making a sacrifice for? Blood would soon flow though, that much was clear. If Fatma and Cemal had sent forth gushes of blood at Sheykh shrine that year, would things have panned out differently?

But Halil continued walking, completely ignorant of such matters. To be fair, nobody else knew anything at that point, either. It was only later that the name of this holy site, even, would be woven into the rumors and hearsay: The proceeds from the tomb belonged to four different villages, the story would go, one of them Our Village, one of them Other Village, and the other two not worth mentioning. That 'blackguard godfather Osman' had for many years been confiscating Other Village's cut of the revenue. That is why there had long been friction between these two families which shared the same surname. That 'brute of a boss Osman' thought his secret was safe, but you can't squeeze a spear into a sack and you can't conceal the truth forever.

High noon was an hour away as Other Village came into view. Halil smiled and glanced over his shoulder to see just how far he had come, but everything was blurry. He could see no farther than a hundred meters. In the opposite direction, up ahead, Other Village stood out clear as day.

When the 'Welcome to Other Village' sign came into view, he felt a slap, a sting, out of nowhere. Then there was a pop and a bang! No, that was the rat-a-rat of the bullets dancing just behind his brand-new leather shoes. Jokey bullets, sure. But this wasn't funny. 'Creepy Osman' always springs out on you like an evil spirit or jinn. He wouldn't leave tracks if he walked in the snow.

Osman and the guy next to him were grinning like roasted sheep skulls. Both of them were smirking, but only one of them was doing the talking. 'Got a problem?' said a voice eager to cause one. Halil hopped up and down as he ran his hand along hair carefully plastered back with lemon juice, as though to keep it from standing on end. He nodded and greeted Osman first, then the other guy. In what passed for a smile, Osman's lip curled back to expose a sinister wasteland of tobacco-stained teeth. The middle ends of his thick eyebrows bumped into each other, forming an endless black horizon. As always, his hands were shaking. Nobody liked him in Our Village.

OSMAN

Osman was an alcoholic. He'd picked up the habit as a teen. And every day since, his breath has reeked of *rakı*. And every day since he married Zennur, she has failed to smile. And every day like clockwork, he has beaten his long-stem rose of a hazel-eyed wife, along with their six children, the youngest three years old, the oldest fifteen. After downing the demon drink, he bashes them all, one after another. He and the commander were tight, so he thought he was untouchable. As long as he did not kill her, there was no problem; she belonged to him. Sixteen years earlier, nobody knows how, he had managed to cobble together the 150,000 lira for the bride price. There were firearms for the big brothers and gold by the kilo for the bride-to-be. In these parts, a bride is only as precious as the gold coins pinned to her gown, the gold necklaces draped round her neck and the gold bracelets slipped onto her wrists. When Osman agreed to the price, Zennur's father paid no mind to his future son-in-law's gold teeth, thicket of black brow, or his shaky hands; he was a distant relative, after all. After the incident, it was said that Zennur had been 'fooling around' with a fellow from Our Village, someone from Leyla's side of the family. That's the term they use here, and it is considered a terrible thing. Four of the six children were supposedly not Osman's at all, but from that fellow in Our Village. At the trial, Mister Prosecutor had requested a paternity test and it really did turn out that one of the children wasn't Osman's, and that therefore it was an 'Our Villager'. The two families were already feuding and this matter of honor was the last straw, is what they said later. Others said it was a lie. A woman from around here gets caught cheating on her husband and doesn't get stabbed in the heart, doesn't have a noose placed round her fair neck, isn't thrown into a well, or found floating face down in a stream... 'Do you really think it would have a happy ending, irreconcilable differences and a matter-of-fact divorce? Don't make us laugh!' they said. 'They're making up this story so Osman can get off light on honor killing charges.'

During Halil's deposition the prosecutor asked if, at the entrance to Other Village on the morning of the incident, the person firing off bullets with Osman was his younger brother, Salih. 'It could have been him,' Halil said. 'The person, whoever it was, resembled Osman,' he added: 'He, too, had a single black line eyebrow and a bushy mustache. He might have been a little shorter, but wiry like his big brother, if not so quick on his feet.'

The prosecutor asked that question for a reason. After the incident, three people from Other Village all swore that Salih had been on duty that morning. Had someone really been with Osman that morning, and if so, who? Not that this information would change anything. The statements were all a mass of contradictions, every one of them. It was no stretch of imagination to assume that Salih would do whatever Osman said. If ordered to do so, he would have left his post. Was Salih a wolf in sheep's clothing? Or was he a crow who, in following a partridge, has forgotten how to walk on the straight and narrow? His wife Havva was disgusted by the sight of Osman. And terrified, too. Whenever he roared for her to bring some tea she would say, 'All right, brother, sir,' and not a word more before rushing to the kitchen. She was a nimble-fingered woman, able to roll out pastry and pop it in the oven first thing in the morning or middle of the night. But she would leave the tray of food and drink in front of her brother-in-law and flee as though from a contagious disease. Havva was not yet thirty. She had three children, aged one, three and six. Who knew how many more would come? Everyone here is born to their fate.

Halil was different, though. You would think he was the son of an Istanbul pasha who happened to be passing through Our Village and would certainly not be spending the night. So well-mannered; such a little lord. He was slender and tall. He had a pleasant face and a Roman nose, hooked and noble, like Mehmet the Conqueror's. He was as stylish as anyone in any village. Never forgotten was the sting of a slap delivered by his father when he said he wanted to be a barber. Nonetheless, Halil clung to that dream. What's more, he wanted to be a barber for women, not men, and in a village of all places. Halil's aspirations and what was left of his wits would have been beaten right out of him were it not for his mother, who flew at her husband with shouting, 'You made me beg for three days for a hospital but took the boy instead to that sultan, or sheykh, or whatever you call it, and a lot of good it did, too, so either butt out and let the boy do what he wants or keep having at him, but do it over my dead body!' For only the second time in her life, Gülüm was standing up to Hasan. And it worked. He lowered his bunched-up fist, cussed something awful and beat it to the coffee house. From that day forward, he was always hands-off with Halil.

OTHER VILLAGE

When Osman popped up like a poisonous mushroom that morning, Halil pursed his full lips. He was peeved.

'Good morning,' he said. 'Where are you gentlemen off to?'

Hollow-cheeked Osman roared with laughter. As did the guy next to him. The pair of them, in matching pinstripe trousers, mafia-style, were simultaneously bent double and slapping their knees. Halil's face clouded over. He took a step toward jug-eared Osman and plucked up the courage to grab him by the shoulders, give him a friendly shake and ask what was so funny; but he missed. The guy's shoulders were like the rest of him, a constantly moving target.

'What are you doing here, shithead?' someone said, and it was Osman again. He lifted his eyebrow, all thoughtful like, when Halil explained about the cologne, and added, 'Get whatever damn thing you need and then get the hell back to your village.'

Other Village was bigger than Our Village, and drier. Even the Gürnehir didn't much like that place. It flows gurgling and sweet along the length of Our Village, only to shudder in its bed and take a sharp shift to the northeast before reaching Other Village. The signs say 'Welcome' but very few are the visitors well-received.

The village crazies–Fahri, Emine, Arif, Sülo and Hatice–had gathered at their usual hang-out by the public fountain. Fahri's urine was aiming a thin yellow stream at the cool water flowing from the tap. Emine was spooning applesauce from a plastic plate to her constant companion, a chicken in a pink bib. Arif was mercilessly pelting passersby from the big bag of rocks at his feet. Sülo had turned his face to the sky and was stuttering a string of creative curses at a hapless bird. Hatice was alternately lisping along to Sülo's latest invented curse and erupting in delighted guffaws and brays. They were a gang of five and always stuck together.

Fish gotta swim and crazies gotta crazy - best get out of here, and quick, Halil decided. Ducking and shielding his head with his hands he picked up his pace and kept walking toward the village square as though nothing was out of the ordinary. Coffee house tables were grouped under a towering sycamore. Ten or twenty men sat there, or it could have been thirty to forty. Two dolls dangled from two branches. The girl doll was dressed in a white wedding gown; the boy in a black suit. Both had beads for eyes. Black beads. Halil asked one of the men what the dolls were doing there.

'What dolls?' the man replied.

'The ones tied to that tree,' Halil said.

He got an expletive for an answer. Halil took another look, really carefully that time, although admittedly it was all a bit blurry, but there were definitely two dolls hanging from two different branches.

Halil spotted his cousin playing backgammon. He's a relative, he'll tell me, Halil thought to himself.

'İbo, why have you gone and tied those dolls to the tree?'

'What tree?' asked İbo, eyes on the board, with a roll of the dice.

What a careless, bloodless bunch they are, Halil was thinking as he headed once again for the grocer's, which was only one or two hundred meters away, this being a village, after all.

Up ahead, a couple of uniformed military police strutted along in tandem; their weapons in their right hands, their legs wide apart, as befits the creators of these mountains and plains endowed with the power of life and death and answerable to no one. As Halil passed them he thought it prudent to wish the two commanders a good morning.

'Think you're funny, do you?' one of them yelled. 'You little bastard!' and they came at Halil.

'God forbid, commanders, I swear I didn't mean anything, I'm just here to get some cologne and I'll be gone before you know it...' is what he would have said if the soldier on the right had not knocked the wind out of him with a rifle butt to the gut. For the second time that morning, Halil found himself sprawled on the ground. When the same soldier shouted,

'Get up and get lost, shithead, before I splatter that bird brain of yours!' Halil's leather soles scrammed along with the rest of him. Around here, if a soldier decides to tell a villager the sky is orange, the correct response is,

'Yes sir, orange sir, commander sir!'

Clearly, there was no peace to be had in this village, but Halil was determined not to be the proverbial mule so new to the job that it unloads its burden while still at the doorway. He would get the job done right, no matter what. Not to mention that if he turned up in Our Village unburdened by ten bottles of cologne he would be skinned alive by his Aunt Fatma.

When he finally got to the grocer's, soaked in sweat, the clock on the wall showed two o'clock. My how the time had flown since he set foot in Other Village. It was there that fortune smiled on him for the first time that morning: Ten bottles and more were there to be had.

'Ten is enough,' Halil said.

Pale Kadri asked if he were buying them for that evening's event. Everyone knows everything. Nothing happens in this place without the knowledge of the village head, the chief of the village guards and the military police. And that is what was so strange about the incident. The second anyone heard, they tried to pin it on the guerrillas. They said it wasn't true that Osman's father had disappeared in an unsolved case: had gone off to the mountains, and from there carried on directing his eight kids. Some asked how the state did not know this and others said the state knew, of course, but was happy to sit back and let them all kill each other. Does the state not supply arms and cash for others to do its dirty deeds? Does it not send local guards ahead in the mountains and in skirmishes, supposedly to act as guides but in reality to serve as bait? Some pointed out that it takes ten minutes, tops, to drive to Our Village from the gendarme station at the entrance to Other Village. Why, they wondered, did it take the military police two hours to show up at the house where the engagement ceremony was held? Was the commander trying to protect someone? And what about the commander's wife, Sehla? Two days before the incident she had gone off to the city with a broken foot, her excuse to get leave from her job at Our Village's primary school. Someone interrupted to say that the schoolteacher was the wife of the sergeant major, not the commander; it comes to the same thing, someone else replied. Another one said that the husband of the schoolteacher in Our Village was an ordinary sergeant and that the lady teacher had not broken her foot but had gone back to her hometown to attend a wedding. Two women from Other Village called the local newspaper to say that they were certain they had seen the teacher the morning of the incident buying peas at the village market. The paper did not find the claim credible enough to print. On their heads be it.

FISH

Pale Kadri slid the ten bottles of cologne into a strong plastic bag. Halil strode past the coffeehouse with his head down. He was burning with thirst but this was no place to stop; the crazies were still at the fountain, still doing whatever it was they were doing that morning. Halil's shock of slicked hair was losing the battle; the sun was now scorching his skull along with everything else. Added to his misery were the grumbling protests of his empty belly. The last chance for a bit of a rest and a bite to eat before hitting the dusty road was that out-of-the-way trout farm of Osman's.

Taking a turn off the main road, Halil walked a few hundred meters, then down a hill and into the farm.

He found it more deserted than usual, despite the tourism season being in full swing. Seeing that there were no customers, it was hard to explain those swollen bank accounts. Somebody, somehow, was making a killing. But other than guard duty, this farm and restaurant was their only known livelihood. After the incident, somebody said you could tell a fat-eating dog from the shine of its coat. They must have been selling drugs and pimping women; selling to whoever bought, whether mafioso, guerrilla or military commander, and somebody ended up paying the price. That is what was said; but who knows if it was true? There is no wealth without wickedness, no fast talk without lies.

Halil settled in under a sun shade at the table for four by the fish pool nearest the entrance. He stretched out his long legs and leaned against the back of an orange chair. Now if he could only find a way to ease his head... the throbbing between his ears since morning was now aggravated by his hunger and the heat. He cradled his head between his hands and rocked it like a baby, but the pain persisted. And as he rocked, the fish seemed to grow livelier, wriggling in the pool, swimming silver and multiplying without knowing that in five minutes or a few days they would be gasping, gutted and grilled before landing on a plate.

It's a nice place. The farm backs up against a hill, and there are trees within and without, to the left and to the right. Green leafy trees. The only thing spoiling the view is the watchtower of the police station. Do the young conscripts sent here from all across Anatolia get hungry when they catch a whiff of fried fish? Those were the thoughts of sensitive Halil as he forgot all about his own troubles. A few families were having lunch in the little open-sided roofed huts lining the road. Each family had three or four children. Halil wanted to have at least five with Maral; boys or girls, makes no difference as long as they're healthy... A little boy was playing with the pump near Halil's table. Water spurted out whenever he pressed the blue handle. Each time, the boy was delighted and amazed. That's kids for you.

And then Osman's beautiful wife Zennur appeared. Halil was taken aback. They don't like their wives to be out in front of people like this, so they must be going through a bad patch. It was later said that the cooks and workers had not been paid a penny in wages for months. A few complaints were made, but what good did it do in a village without a union? Everyone knew the military police were on the side of the employers, but the workers still gave it a try, and got nothing for their trouble. As a last resort they started to come late, work slow and then not show up at all some days. So that must have been why that poor woman, the beautiful Zennur, showed up at the restaurant with a bruised face. There was even some blood still under her left eye. Rotten-to-the-core Osman had beaten her again. What was Zennur to do without anyone for protection? Her father would not take her back. She was stained; damaged goods. That's what they say around here, and it is terrible.

Speaking through the little white tent over her mouth formed by her muslin head covering, Zenne asked, '*Ayran* or cola, Halil?'

Now *ayran* doesn't go with fish, but that is what Halil hankered after, and he asked for an icy one. If either the yogurt or fish isn't fresh, you get food poisoning, or so they said on the news the other day. But surely nothing bad could come of either the fish squiggling right before his eyes or some homemade yogurt whisked into *ayran*. Halil had no sooner downed a tall foamy glass of the stuff when a boy of ten or so set a fresh tea down in front of him. He must have been one of Osman's kids. Not that he took after him. The sweet smile and green eyes could only have come from Zennur.

The *ayran* and tea were enough to stop Halil's head from spinning, at least. A second tea was followed by a salad loaded with onions. After a vigorous shake of salt, he dug in. He salted everything without tasting it first. He's got no time for sweets, but he loves his salt. And hot spices, too. Everyone here does. Even the fish placed on his table was marinated in a fiery pepper sauce. It was nicely grilled with just the right touch of crispiness. If his mother could see him now, after all those whacks with a stick for not finishing his supper, she would shed tears of joy. He put the whole meal away in less than ten minutes. And had another round of reddish–or rabbit blood–tea, as they called it. It was all so tasty to Tall Halil. With not one, but two, servers rushing about over him. Then he did a double take. Who knew Zennur had a sister so like her? Halil said to himself. He was seeing her for the first time.

MARAL

Maral held up the dark green *entari*, carefully laid it out on the low couch and studied it with eyes of honey. The modest V-neck dipped to just above the bosom. The sleeves extended past the wrist to the middle of the hand. There were tiny slits along the sides of the pinkie fingers; whoever had thought to make those slits in the sleeve had thought well. The waist was gathered and the skirt flared ever so slightly all the way to the floor, for a princess effect. She had tried on this robe countless times and was always left ecstatic by the fabric's flow from the waist down. On the dark green were big black roses. Maral particularly liked that they were black; it was different. She was going to wear her big hoop earrings of gold. Halil always called her golden eyes. She had laughed the first time he said it, when they were eight, playing Five Stones in the street. Halil had been losing again, so that Maral could win. Her honey eyes, so like her mother's, were trained on Halil in a look that said, "Oh, come on, whoever heard of eyes of gold," and then her smile showed milk teeth of mother-of-pearl. When Maral smiles, her right cheek gives a kind of wink. And it was that knowing dimple, those honey-gold eyes and that pearl of a smile that Halil had been in love with ever since. Here, hearts pine for the daughter of a father's brother, or the son of a mother's sister. From time to time, Halil would reproach his mother, asking her why she hadn't arranged a crib contract with Maral. It was not unheard of for babies to become engaged and then married when they came of age. Each time, his mother would soothe him, telling him it would happen one day, and not to worry. Well, how could she have known what was in the stars? How was she to know that on that star-crossed night, Maral, honey-eyed Maral, would try to comfort her little brother Nisar with the words 'my golden eyes,' and that Halil would mourn Maral with those same words.

All of a sudden, yet another uproar broke out at the neighbours'. Leaving her robe on the couch, Maral rushed outside. As calm as the house to their right was–which was no surprise, considering its inhabitants were 90-year-old Granny Berze and 37-year-old Aunt Nasibe–the one to their left was equally as raucous. Compared to the roomy, two-storey house with courtyard nicely surrounded by a stone wall that Maral and her family called home, the dwelling next door stood out like a stunted stepchild. Eight children were growing up in that house. The minute Maral stepped into the street, she saw one of them in the form of Davut and his scratched face, bawling as he ran straight toward her. Davut was only five. If climbing trees, hiding at meal times and shattering the odd window with a slingshot was naughty, then, yes, he was a naughty boy. Beggar dervishes never get their fill of wedding feasts and children never tire of games. But try explaining that to Zozan, the boy's mother. She was a woman on the larger side. And to pound a boy that tiny with fists that big was something nobody, let alone a mother, should ever do.

The children had been left to the tender mercies of their mother when their father, Dilaver, died in a skirmish the previous year. But the monthly cheque from the state was enough to keep body and soul together, the eldest daughter had been married for nine or ten years and the older children had long been chipping in what they could. The family had a roof over its head and food in their bellies, but Zozan's rage never subsided. She, too, was walloped as a child; everybody makes mistakes. That is what Maral's mother, Fatma, said one day as Maral sobbed and spread some salve on Davut's skinny arms bruised by pinches and bites. But Maral's tender, young mind was having none of it.

'So what?' she said. 'If she knows how terrible it is, why do it to her own children?'

But there you go; some things are baked in the cake.

Davut, dark-eyed Davut, opened his arms wide and hugged Maral as if he had stumbled across water in the desert. Maral, with her slim body and big heart, provided a gentle presence and a shelter of sorts for the village children; she was more tigress than doe, which is what her name meant. She left Davut to himself for a moment so he could cry out the tears of a boy without a father and so the fury could flow out of his fists. Then she led him into her home, to the kitchen, where she spread mulberry molasses on a fresh hunk of bread. When Nisar waddled in and hugged Davut, those fists and kicks and punches were soon forgotten.

But there was a drum in Maral's belly. One of calfskin. Swollen and pounding. In her fourteen years on earth, Maral had never felt anything like it. There is sound advice behind the saying, better to leave a task for the morning than to do it in the black of night; when the day turned and the dark descended, those sounds in her belly would multiply.

And that intrusive marching band continued to thump out its ominous music, but Auntie Nasibe had appeared in the doorway.

'Maral, are you waiting for an invitation?' she asked, both in reproach and jest. 'We've still got 30 houses to visit. Even though everyone already knows they are invited, it is customary to visit each and every house on the morning of an engagement feast to confirm to one and all that their presence is welcomed and expected.'

Maral gave Davut and Nisar a peck on the cheek, left her house slippers inside and headed for the door, just outside of which was a rack from which she could select a pair of shoes. Her aunt had already walked back through the courtyard and beyond the blue iron door, where she was gabbing with somebody in the street. Maral chuckled to herself. Her aunt, usually so quiet, could chat up a storm when the spirit moved her; well, sharing a home with Granny, who was not always all there, must make the poor thing feel like a chained snowy owl at times. The little indentation in her cheek turned into a dimple, that tell-tale sign she was inwardly amused. She was poised to step outside when a gust of wind slammed the door in her face with a bang. Bang! Her heart leapt to her mouth. The band in her belly reached a crescendo, drowning out her thoughts.

She pushed against the door; it would not open. As though there were ten men on the other side, and all ten were leaning their combined weight against it. Face drained of colour, she recited, 'In the name of God, the most Gracious, the most Merciful...' and tried again. It would not open. Another recitation, and this time the door swung open, all at once, released by ten men, with a bang! She nearly tumbled to the ground. There was a buzzing. A cloud of dust. A sandstorm striking out of nowhere. Her eyes and mouth filling with fine sand, she called out to her aunt; there was no answer. Called again; nothing. She made to go back inside; this time the twenty hands of ten men pulled with all their might from inside the house, on the other side of the door and she was standing on the threshold; no slippers, no shoes, barefoot.

She felt a gust of wind on her face; a jinn-like presence. And it was then that she, a girl nearly old enough to get married, began screaming at the top of her lungs. Her mother came running out of the kitchen, out of breath and asking, 'What's wrong? What's wrong?'

Maral nestled her head against motherly softness and cried her eyes out, for a moment more orphan than Davut, more toddler than Nisar. Her mother Fatma put the tears down to Leyla's engagement and the looming loss of a big sister. She consulted her own sister, Nasibe, on whether it was wise to make the poor girl go door-to-door all morning. As the two women whispered together, Maral lifted her head, wiped her eyes and saw that the sun was out again and everything was back to normal; everything, that is, but the bitter grains of sand in her mouth and the burning in her throat. She was already feeling sheepish over the cologne; the engagement was taking place in her house; the bride-to-be was her sister; the duty of making the rounds with Nasibe was hers and hers alone.

'Okay,' her mother said, 'but come have a glass of water first, my lamb, and what's so scary about a little sandstorm, anyway?'

As the water flowed from the faucet like a river rushing to reunion with the sea, a proverb came to Fatma's mind, right out of the blue, something that her late father Bozo had often repeated. Yes, that imposing, fearless and kind father of hers would often say: Never sweep walnuts in the moonlight. Which made absolutely no sense to Fatma until she was old enough to learn that stubborn walnuts are swept off high branches with long poles, an undertaking both futile and dangerous in the dark of night, moon or not. There really is a time and a place for everything. The smile on Fatma's face faded as her unease grew. A black-mawed worm was worrying her deep inside. She spun round once, spun round twice, told herself that rains and storms were no cause to cancel an engagement ceremony, and sat back down.

LEYLA

If Leyla's hair was the night, her face was the sun. She had spent the entire week cleaning the darkest corners of the house, and not a spider on the ceiling nor a beetle in the kitchen survived her efforts. Her limbs were worn-out, her spirits buoyant.

Leyla's mother Fatma had marshaled a crew of women that included her youngest sister Nasibe, as well as her two older sisters, Rahime and Hatice, along with their daughters. They all pitched in to prepare the house for the evening, as though it were the house, rather than Leyla, who was to be married off in a few weeks. Leyla's family had the biggest, most impressive home in Our Village, and there were chores galore for these women whose married life was never without a stick on the back and a baby in the womb; these women who lit the stove before sunrise, cracked corn for bread, milked the cow, labored in the field, nursed the baby, swept the floor, satisfied the husband in the bedroom and gradually became experts in the art of survival as they completed an impossible workload every single day on four or five hours of sleep. Had they been celebrities, that evening's event would have been dubbed 'the engagement of the year'. But as it turned out, the night would be featured not in glossy magazines but as breaking news, before being hushed up with the quiet connivance of the family elders, the village leaders and the state—until, finally, it was completely forgotten.

Leyla's mountain-moving mother Fatma assigned particular importance to the divanhane being spic and span, with its cushions and pillows pummeled and aired until they smelled of spring and its windows wiped down until speck-free to even the sharpest eye. The divanhane was the house's showcase, its medal of honor, its crowning touch; there was no shame in letting it proclaim that this was a family with deep pockets, full bellies and heads held high.

Leyla's mother Fatma, who could extract milk from a billy goat if she put her mind to it, was supervising the activities in the kitchen that morning. A dinner feast for at least eighty was being prepared. Large rocks were found and brought to the courtyard, where fire pits were constructed. Kindling was stacked within each grouping of four rocks and crackling fires were lit. The children were treated to sliced bread slathered with yogurt, and sent off to the street so that none of them would end up like Deaf Azimet's son Eyüp, the poor little tyke pulled half-dead from the embers at Döne and Bayram's wedding dinner the year before. Over the shameless mouths of the insatiable flames rested cauldrons big enough to contain a baby. Into a few of them were tossed chunks taken from only the most fragrant and choice hunks of sheep and lamb. The remainder would cook up a pilaf made with long-grain rice grown in the rich volcanic soil of Mount Masia. The cases of yellow and black cola bought in Town two days earlier were being kept chilled in the fridges of friends and neighbours. Leyla's father Cemal had gone off to Town in the morning to pick up his order of baklava from Butterball Hasan, the pastry chef whose fingers dripped sweet goodness. To keep the baklava safe from stumbling children and daytime nibblers, tray after tray of it was covered with tablecloths and carefully hidden away in the large ground floor room—across from the divanhane and next to the kitchen—where the women would be gathering that evening.

As her quick-fingered mother toiled in the courtyard, Leyla went upstairs. After the divanhane, the rooftop terrace was the most important place in the house. There, the men would eat. The terrace had been scrubbed down with sweet-smelling liquid soap by hands red and raw, and it now needed a final sweep. Leyla first checked to make sure that the weathered wooden ladder leading to the rooftop had withstood the heat and damp and could support the weight of scores of sturdy, strong men. The rungs all seemed sound enough. She rested the ladder on the wider side of the courtyard next to Zozan's house; the lopsided outdoor areas of Our Village houses lacked the perfect proportions of homes and gardens in the city. When her father had the house built 20 years earlier, he had decided against a permanent concrete staircase that children could climb at will. The misfortune of Mad Hüso—the son of Fatma's big sister Hatice—a year previously had been a warning for the entire village. At the age of seven, Hüso, who was born with a plank missing, had climbed the concrete steps proudly installed by his father Ahmet, and, for reasons unknown, leapt off the rooftop, landing on his head and dying on the spot. A few months earlier, the boy's fifteen-year-old brother İbrahim had ended up at the police station, again, for reasons unknown. He appeared the following day with a crooked nose and a bloodied lip. After that, 'people' were added to the roster of terrifying characters tormenting poor Mad Hüso day and night, right up there with ghosts and goblins, one-eyed imps and three-headed ogres, redheaded demons and the black-clawed bogeymen. Only much later did a neighbour reveal that on the day Mad Hüso died, İbrahim, the big brother he adored, was seen running from the military police. Mad Hüso climbed the concrete stairs, went onto the rooftop, shouted, and jumped up and down to distract the long arm of the law. But the father Ahmet, who was a village guard, fiercely denied it all, insisting that İbrahim only become entangled in that one bit of monkey business a few months previously, for which the boy got a good whacking from his father, when he got home from the police station, and never, ever, had there been another incident that could bring shame on the family. In the end, nobody ever found out why Mad Hüso fell from the roof or exactly why İbrahim was taken to the police station; but who among us would admit that our *ayran* is sour?

Viewed from the flat roof of the two-storey house, Our Village was a paradise to Leyla's eyes. There was no endless sea under sailing ships, no forests brimming with a thousand

and one curious creatures, no fertile plains disappearing into the horizon, like the villages to the south, and no encircling of protective mountains to shield wife and child from wolf and savage beast, like the villages to the east. It was as though a small tract of land, a little green and a little yellow, a little flat and a little hilly, with not much water, but enough to go around, had been plopped down in the middle of nowhere and the people of Our Village were free to take it or leave it; but raven-haired Leyla loved it nonetheless. 'When we marry, let me take you to Upper City, and we'll live there,' Bilal had said. He had two shops there, at Aynalı Han, but Leyla pushed back. She was also too attached to her mother to leave. Now her eyes welled up and she thought, for a moment, that she was overcome with emotion until she realized it was sand filling her eyes. A powerful cloud of dust arising out of nowhere pushed Leyla toward the satellite dish in the right-hand corner connecting Our Village to the wider world. She tried to beat it back with her arms, to beat back this sudden jinn-like force, to free herself from whatever it was. She screwed her eyes shut, locked her hands together and recited every prayer that came to mind. A few minutes later, she dared to open her eyes and looked down to see if the sand had put out the fires. No, everything was in place, everybody was calm and at work, as though nothing at all had happened. Perhaps it was just her nerves. And was it not true that later nobody would say with any certainty or credibility exactly what and what not had happened? One of the old-timers from Our Village, now living in Bursa, would say to the reporter that tracked him there: 'As you know, the killers and the killed shared the same last name. Back in the day, these two families showed up in Our Village; hirelings, we called them, and they had nothing to their name. We in the village, on the other hand, were all related, six households. They got into a power struggle with us and went so far as to kill one of our family elders. We took the life of one of theirs in retaliation, one of that gang leader Osman's ancestors. This was the eighties... even back then, some of us, fearing a blood feud, packed up and left. That captain with the dog at his side rounded up 18 of our men, young and old, and put them through the wringer. Some more of us went west after that, to Bursa, to İzmir, to Mersin... Later, in the nineties, the District Head told those of us remaining behind to become village guards, but we said no. When we refused, he made the same offer to the hirelings; some of them agreed on the spot, others waited a few years; but they all became village guards. And that is when those of us still left in the village, me included, had to migrate. Our fields were valuable, well-watered. They grabbed them all without shame. The killed seized most of them, causing ill-will with the killers. That's what this is all about. What I say is that they killed each other over land that didn't belong to either of them in the first place; never expect a fix from poison or fidelity from a whore.'

But well before this interview in Bursa, a lavish dinner was being laid out. The men would sit opposite each other in two long lines, cross-legged. On the spotless tablecloth before them would be placed platters, one per four men. There would be tender meat and steaming rice. Leyla's was a leading family, and the chunks would be large and choice. The men's portions would be bigger than the women's, of course. In the approaching twilight of late dusk, guests would stream through the courtyard entrance and to the main door of the house, where they would put their shoes on the rack. The very shoe rack that in a few hours would be splattered with blood.

MARAL

Süleyman's boy, Satan Emir, appeared in the doorway. Of all the people to answer the door, why him? Maral was thinking. And that nickname, too, was so unfair; there's nothing satanic about the poor little guy. None of the family's five children were 'all there', not as the offspring of parents whose mothers' sisters were each other's aunts; but Emir was the least lucky of them all. His foot was twisted backward from birth. When the midwife saw the emergence of not a head but a foot, and that foot no less, she ran off screaming, 'I'm not birthing Satan and you can't make me!' That's when the women living nearby rolled up their sleeves to get the job done; after all, their combined experience was equal not only to a midwife, but to ten doctors. Pushing and pulling, working all together, the baby was delivered, but the mother died of blood loss. The tag 'Satan' stuck to the boy, even after his father Süleyman, by all accounts a religious man who believed that it was God's commandment his son be deformed and his wife dead, chose the name 'commandment', which, in the language of the Koran, is 'Emir'. As Satan Emir grew up, he could not decide which was worse, the absence of a mother or the constant abuse from the children who chased him with shouted taunts of 'devil-boy, mother-killer, dirty Emir, devil Emir, here Emir, there Emir', all the while pelting him with sticks, stones, bugs, worms, and whatever else they got their hands on.

With a maturity beyond his ten years–a motherless devil spawn grows up fast–Emir, little Satan Emir, greeted Maral and Nasibe that morning with the calculated combination of warmth, courtesy and respect generally delivered by the man of the house: 'I'm the only one at home right now. Father is on guard duty this evening and won't be able to come. If you wish, I will attend.'

It is a small place. In less than twenty-five minutes they had visited fourteen houses. By then they were thirsty; it being an unusually hot spring day in Our Village. Answering the fifteenth door was Lovely Avşin, Serdal's second wife. Avşin from Other Village. She was sixteen years old. Gazing upon Maral and her aunt with eyes whose flecks were the fresh green of new shoots–Serdal's description at their first encounter–she invited Maral and her aunt inside. And inside they went. Nasibe, who normally could not stomach social interactions, darted through the doorway in no time flat, so anxious was she to see her friend Medine. Not that there was much to see: Serdar's legally wedded wife was ten years Nasibe's junior, and an invalid. Upon her failure to produce a child, Serdal had brought home a second wife to keep his bloodline from drying up. What else was he to do? A barren woman is a sunless summer, a waterless stream, a starless sky, a roofless house. The widespread intermarriage in Our Village made polygamy scarce; but in this case, it was necessary. Serdal was a man, after all, and he chose a wife who was both young and lovely. He himself was not a pretty sight and could never win Avşin's heart; but the choice was not hers to make. The word of men, the state and God was final, if not always in that order. Resignation to one's fate was the only path available to everyone else. When Avşin's father decided to sell her–that's what they say here, and it's a terrible term–Serdal paid the hefty bride price, even selling off his field to raise the cash. Lovely of lovelies Avşin cried her eyes out day and night in protest of her pending marriage, but to no avail. Her mother Masum, too, was against it, but little did that matter, either. Avşin's father and uncle had made their decision, and there was no turning back. 'And anyway,' they said, 'she has come of age. We've taught her to read and write, and it's not like she's going to go off and become a schoolteacher. It is decided; this is her kismet; we are giving her to Serdal.'

'Listen up, Avşin, if you produce a boy, your husband has promised to sacrifice a ram.' That is what her father said.

'We are born with our fate inscribed on our foreheads; Allah has willed it, so try to be happy, my girl; listen when I tell you that the way to avoid suffering is not to sadden your husband, not to anger him, not to stray from his word.' That is what her mother said.

But Lovely Avşin immediately forgot her mother's advice and duly received a good slap from her husband on their first night together in Our Village. 'Am I such an ogre that you fear me? Am I such a leper that I disgust you? Choose a horse already made and a wife in the making, is what I say. If I ever see you crying again, out you go.' That is what her husband said.

Were she thrown out, Avşin would have nowhere to go. She said nothing, and sat down.

That day, Nasibe made a beeline for the floor mat in the corner on which her friend lay smelling for all the world like a rag that after a long day's use as a cleaning cloth has been cast aside unrinsed and still damp. 'It's the drugs that did it to her,' Nasibe said aloud.

'So it seems,' Lovely Avşin agreed. 'I, too, am terribly sorry for Sister Medine; who would ever want to be in such a state,' said Lovely Avşin.

'Medine fell into a deep well when she couldn't conceive, and she's been there ever since,' said Nasibe. 'When First Wife Medine was unable to get up even to serve her husband, they took her to the hospital in Upper City. I was with her that day. There was a line all the way from the hospital to the supplier's at the end of the street, and so crowded were the corridors that they were moving patients outside. The doctor gave her a quick look-over and wrote a prescription. We helped her take her medicine. But Medine continued to take to her bed like they'd covered her back in glue. So we took her to the doctor in Upper City a few more times. Each time, he prescribed a different medicine. That's when I said to Serdal, I said, all these drugs are going to do her more harm than good; but who listens to me, anyway? The last one is what did it. My friend was never the same. She came down with something one night and never got up again.'

And as Nasibe talked, Lovely Avşin sobbed in silence, the forbidden tears streaming down her cheeks. Pearls.

'Well, my friend is lucky to have you to look after her, at least, so God bless you, Avşin, but I do believe she's gone and soiled herself again, and what a terrible smell it is, too,' said Nasibe.

'Sister, I just changed her diaper, but the stink won't go away, though I bathe her every day. So Serdal won't be disgusted and, well, you know what he's like; we wouldn't want him to toss the poor woman out into the street, now would we,' said Lovely Avşin.

And at that moment, Maral, who was sitting on the low couch by the window, looking outside as she listened, felt that thrum-thrumming again, that drum in her belly. A second sight somewhere deep in her gut suspected that this stink, too, was a sign, one both sinister and sad. Her eyes now trained on Lovely Avşin, compelled to watch her every move, Maral was thinking how this young woman was only two years her senior: Tall and slender, with long delicate hands and white skin, Avşin was truly lovely to the eye. Yet against her will she had been torn from her mother, without her consent she had been married off, and before she knew it, she had been brought here, to this house, to care for a bedridden woman while trying to give a man an heir.

Maral's father Cemal was different; surely, he would never allow that to happen to his own daughter. Her Uncle

Mahmut had wanted her big sister Leyla for his middle son, but her father had said that the girl's heart wouldn't allow it and neither would he. A refusal under these circumstances was virtually unheard of here, where to be wedded with the son of an uncle was to have the most desirable pairing imaginable, keeping unchanged as it does the power dynamic within the family and the property which they share. Those were Maral's thoughts, but nobody knew the truth of the matter, for who listens to a girl? It was a mystery why Cemal chose to give Leyla not to his elder brother's son, but to a nephew on his wife's mother's side of the family. Later, one of the suspects would toss out an allegation shedding some light on this. According to him, two months earlier someone in Cemal's family had raped someone in the uncle's family. And the girl, Leyla, was then offered up to the middle son to make amends. But then, not only did Cemal renege on the deal, he rubbed it in by giving Leyla to a relative of Fatma's–to a boy from a family with which the uncle and his family were already entangled in a long-running feud. They were warned to break off the engagement plans, told there would be a heavy price to pay; but they did not listen. And wouldn't you know it, at the next hearing that same suspect would repudiate his earlier testimony and be tossed out of the courthouse by the prosecutor. An ancient villager was at least able to confirm the dispute between the two sides. There really was a blood feud between Osman's clan and that of Fatma's mother, Berze; a dispute dating back to the nineties. The two sides had clashed over picnic and recreation areas, resulting in two separate murders. Everyone knew this, but nobody ever talked about it, the ancient villager explained.

By the time Maral and Aunt Nasibe had finished sipping their water and tea it was past noon, so they stopped only briefly at the next 15 houses. Some women were making yogurt and others aged sheep's cheese; some were pounding wheat into bulgur and others, in groups of ten and twenty, were outside gathered around a clay oven baking bread. There were kitchens sending forth the usual aromas of white beans stewed with diced meat and tomato, of *tırşık*, of lentil and of trotter soup; and from the houses welcoming honored guests that day came the special scents of *sembusek*, of stuffed ribs, of cinnamon-scented pilaf with lamb liver.

They knocked on the last door. Number 31. Tucked away at the top of a dirt road leading to the highway two kilometres away, this house was next to Our Village's cemetery. Accursed Esma answered on the first knock. She smiled at the sight of Maral and Nasibe; Esma had few visitors, you see. Her husband Derviş, the son of her father's brother, was a village guard like all the other men, but he and his family's blood ties to the other people of Our Village were tenuous, so he and his family were viewed as relative outsiders. There were nine children in that house, and all nine were girls: and this was only the beginning of Esma's curse. To some fall a melon sweet; to others fall a melon green. Three daughters had been sent off with husbands; three were in primary school; three awaited a match. Some said that in the days and months before the arrival of her last baby, Esma had prayed that if it be a girl, it be born dead, and that an aggrieved God had then given her the girl she got. The reason, if there was one, for the stricken state of that baby would never be known, but it was a fact that Maral always needed to run to the comfort of her mother's arms after a glimpse of baby number nine, of Jinn-Jinxed Raziye; otherwise, she was unable to sleep, would wake up screaming from nightmares, alarming her family. On one of those nights, her father, thinking a guerrilla raid was underway, reached in his sleep for his rifle, and when Fatma awoke him with a slap to the face realized he was pointing the muzzle at Maral. Husband and wife decided together that from that night on Maral would sleep with her mother after each and every sighting of Jinn-Jinxed Raziye. Wolf and sheep, worry and sleep, do not mix. At the very moment Maral was thinking, how lucky for me that that girl is not here, and feeling relieved that she would not need to trouble her mother after such a long, tiring day, she caught sight of Jinn-Jinxed Raziye staring out of the kitchen window to her left. It is a hard thing to say this about a tiny child, but the left half of the girl's face was horribly misshapen, as though jinn-struck.

HALİL

Hunger leads a fox out of the forest and it was to the fish restaurant that it led Halil, who, with a belly now full and a head aching less intensely, gathered his wits, pulled out the watch that had been a present from his father for his birthday the previous year, and checked the time. Noon had turned into evening. The watch was fancy, a Casio. 126 grams. Mineral glass. Waterproof up to 50 meters underwater. Gray-gold case. Gray-gold steel bracelet. Diameter 44.9mm, height 50mm, thickness 9.4mm. Ionized plated, oval case. First and second hands half white gold, half yellow; third hand yellow gold. Of the numerals, only 3, 6, 9 and 12 were permitted an appearance, in white. The rest were simple stick bar markers in yellow gold, hirelings temporarily filling in for field hands out sick. Wind-up mechanism, also of yellow gold. At least the face is black, Halil had said to himself after opening up the box and doing extensive research on the internet. Had he been given his pick of time-pieces, this one would have been far down the list. His would be smaller, with a slim strap and a thinner case, and definitely in gray and black. But his father was obsessed with the glittery stuff, so much so that he had replaced a rotten tooth with a gold one. Halil loved silver. The fine fused wires of *telkari* jewelry, for instance. How could gold possibly compete with rings that were an embroidery of silvery strands, of looping and entwining lovers, once long lost, now reunited; or possibly compare with bracelets yearning to become water droplets and with earrings redolent of the pale luminous flowers of fertility plants? When he married Maral, he would have to follow tradition and hand over kilos of gold, but he would also, whenever possible – on birthdays, anniversaries, Valentine's day, Mother's Day – shower his beloved with *telkari* of all sizes and shapes, with necklaces scattering silver from throat to breast, with a belt whose fine filigree buckle dangled six five-leaf clovers swaying in time as the silver gilt weave wrapped itself round her waist not once, but twice, and with a *Shahmaran* glove of see-through silver mesh showing off the back of her soft hand between bracelet and ring, and more, much more…

He tore his thoughts away from Maral and directed them to the task at hand, the ten bottles of cologne awaiting delivery to his aunt, the mother of his beloved. Sated and satisfied, too, was the sun which, worn out by a long day scorching one and all, chose to conceal its fiery face behind a cloud at the very moment he sprang to his feet with a spinning head. That's what comes of getting up so fast, he groaned as he sank back down on the chair, his legs still shaking. He started counting up to fifty, a tactic he had developed as a very small, and very overwhelmed, child. Counting internally was for when he was dragged off to the houses of relatives on holidays and the hands of elders were thrust at his face so he could kiss them, hands reeking of onions, garlic, manure, tobacco and old age, churning his stomach; or for the times he was rocking back and forth waiting for someone, or something, and got smacked again by Father and told to stop acting like a retard; but the most unbearable sensation of all was the stab of sorrow straight to the heart every time he watched Maral walk home after they finished playing together.

'The caravan straightens itself out on the road,' Tall Halil said aloud, bracing himself before standing up on the count of fifty-one. The ten one-liter plastic containers in the bag were seemingly filled with feathers, not with a mixture of water, alcohol and fragrance. Spurred on by the prospect of seeing Maral, he was back in half an hour flat, thirty minutes less than the trip out. The last three kilometres he ran, past the terrible cemetery and the village graveyard.

Halil heaved a sigh of relief at the 'Our Village' sign. That's funny, he said to himself as he was trying to catch his breath, they've put up a second sign; even the smartest guys around here would put their yogurt through the mill if nobody told them better. It got darker, all at once, and everything became blurry. In the pit of his stomach, like during those feverish nights at Sheykh Shrine, he felt something stir; a spasm, a squeezing pain, wriggling and rising higher. His heart skipped a beat; ever since his granny died just hours after complaints of a stomach ache, he had firmly believed that the spirit emerges from the stomach on its way to the next world.

He was panting when he reached his Aunt Fatma's house. The blue door leading into the courtyard from the street was ajar. The women inside must have finished cooking, for they were putting out the embers, carrying cauldrons to the kitchen and cleaning up. A squad of women toiling as one, worker bees not letting a second go to waste, in a display of precision and discipline that would be the envy of even the flintiest commander. Halil gave them another glance out of the corner of his eye; they were many, a platoon, not a squad. He headed straight for the kitchen. His aunt was there, at the head of the long table, counting as she stacked plates destined for the rooftop feast. Like a novice dervish bursting into the sunlight after forty days and forty nights of self-inflicted suffering, he ran to his aunt.

Fatma smiled at the sight of Halil, that adorably courtly little nephew of hers. He was worn and drained, that much she could see, but there was not the faintest hint of sweat or odor; the young padishah had just returned on his steed, nothing dirtied nor disturbed, save for his slightly tousled thick hair, that was all.

'Get over here, boy, and give me a proper hello and a big hug so I know I'm loved,' she teased.

When Halil missed, embracing with outstretched arms not his aunt, but the air, he was mortified. Putting it down to fatigue after the long walk, his aunt pulled her nephew into her strong stable arms, and he let go of everything pent-up inside. There was no sobbing, no moaning, and certainly no pouring out of troubles; what left his mouth was the involuntary gasp of gratitude for a godsend, the simple sound: 'Oh'.

'I don't know what's going on between the two of you and your overflowing little hearts – bless you both, by the way– but Maral, too, has been acting kind of funny lately, as though she's gone and got herself betrothed without telling anyone, and we can't have that, now can we.'

It was the year of ill fate, and that she did not know.

OSMAN

'Yasin, you drive the truck,' said Sheik Osman. 'Be in front of the house at nine-thirty sharp.'

'Hüseyin, Mehmet, Şükrü; take up your positions, one man each, at the houses of Zozan, Nasibe and Ömer.'

'The three of us–my son İsmail, me and Ramazan–will go to the men.'

'Salih, go to the women with İdris and Mahmut. Don't touch them.'

'If anyone asks during the day, tell them you've got guard duty. Say we'll stop by late, if we can, and not a peep more. There's still time till evening, so get your fill of food and some rest.' And so Osman continued, he who could squeeze blood from a stone and turn a hyena into a vicious wolf.

'Don't let your wives and daughters go to the engagement, any collateral damage, you'll be held accountable,' hissed cold-of-blood, cold-of-heart Osman.

The rain of orders to the men stopped so he could bellow for that 'damn tea' he'd ordered from the woman in the kitchen.

Tall slender Zennur shrank into herself, and in a voice stretched thin she cried, 'I'm bringing it.'

When Zennur came into the divanhane with a round tray of tea and a plate of *kıllor* pastry, ten men buttoned ten pairs of lips. Osman broke the silence with a rebuke:

'Bringing guests tea too much trouble for you, I see,' he said, 'but a smack on the chops will fix that sour face of yours; look here, I handed over a bag of gold for you and I'll be damned if I don't whip you into shape, so count on seeing me later,' he added, glaring at his wife.

Hoping to soften him with her eyes, Zennur lifted her face and forced a jittery smile under white muslin, only to see blackest night in her husband's eyes; those same bottomless pits she saw every time he went off in the dusk to do guard duty. Osman never said a word about any of that to Zennur. It was not that sort of job, and besides, women wouldn't understand; 'long hair, short wits' is what they say in these parts.

'We meet here at eight. Yasin, kick the tires, and good. Fill up the tank and give it a look-over. Make sure the engine and transmission are in tip-top shape. We need the brakes to work, and the fuel flowing through the line and pump. Anything goes wrong with that truck, it's on your head,' warned face-wiped-with-a-butcher's-rag Osman. 'Leave your weapons at home. I'll distribute the hardware.'

The nine heads of nine cowards nodded as one.

After the incident, some said the guards' guns were used and some said the weapons came from the outside. Someone said that the electric igniters, grenades, sticks of dynamite, kalashnikovs and handguns found in a cave on the village outskirts were a smokescreen. On the same day Yasin killed himself, the day before the hearing, Salih called out to one of the prison wardens, saying, 'let me out of this cell, I got a load to get off my chest. We stuck the weapons in the cave,' he then told the head warden, 'and they're as clean as the ones registered for state duty; we buried the real hardware near the road to town, and me and my brother are the only ones who know where.'

But when the prison prosecutor came to get a statement the next day, Salih took it all back.

'You sonuvabitch, you fried my brain with your long-winded story last night, so you better tell the prosecutor what you told me,' the head warden said, 'or, believe me, you'll curse your mother for bringing you into this world; don't forget who's god around here; there's nobody to protect you.'

The prosecutor left empty-handed. Crake and crake, lark and lark; bare-head chick and lame-leg cock: birds of a feather, flocking together.

HALİL

Satan Emir, the first guest to materialize, sat himself down in front of the iron door leading into the house, playing host. His step-mother Dilan, along with his three step-siblings and the four siblings left motherless when he was born, joined him toward eight o'clock. Into the courtyard came other guests, too. The trophies of gold taken out of boxes by married women were gleaming on their wrists and ears, waists and necks; girls' eyelids were shaded in brilliant hues of green and blue, and more vivid still were the shimmering yellows and purples of their floor-length, full-sleeved *fistan*. The elderly women were dignified if indistinct in simple maroon *kofi* over snow-white *kitan*. The girls, meanwhile, poked their confidants in the shoulder, pointed out certain young men on the opposite side of the courtyard, giggled, and blushed over feelings both revealed and concealed, as girls their age will do the world over. It was on nights such as this that a girl might get an approving nod from an elder and a visit on the following day from the parents of a precious son making a formal request for marriage, upon which – but only after much haggling over the bride price, gold jewelry and expensive gifts for the girl's father and brothers – a religious nuptial rite, an engagement and a wedding would all take place one after another over the space of several months, and, almost before the girl knew it, she would be joining the ranks of married women who have learned to embrace their fate with all the serenity of a saint.

The girls and women – and in this place the line dividing the two is as non-negotiable as the line separating life and death – began congregating in the large room across from the divanhane. Children unable to squeeze into the house were out in the courtyard with their watchful big sisters, raising a ruckus. A distracted smile on their faces, Fatma, her big sisters, her little sister, and all of their daughters, were in the kitchen finishing preparations for the feast. Wafting through the entire neighbourhood was the fragrance of pilaf and the occasional whiff of lamb stewed into tender chunks of flesh flavored with the 1001 wild herbs and grasses upon which it had grazed in happier times; in a respite from the funereal laments so often wailed by women and girls in these parts, someone burst into joyful song, bringing forth blossoms of bliss in the souls of the good folk flocking in a little early.

Among them were Zozan and her five children; followed by Fatty Bekir and wife; and Döne, belly swollen again, and so soon, right behind Bayram, the husband absolutely adored as a first cousin before he married her just last year; along with Deaf Azimet, whose husband was on guard duty tonight, and who chose, out of all her six children, to make the piteous point of bringing only Eyüp, the little boy nearly burnt to death at Döne's wedding dinner the previous year; and then there were Accursed Esma and Derviş, expectantly displaying on their arms their middle trio of nubile daughters, having chosen to leave at home Jinn-Jinxed Raziye and the two other little girls. Of the thirty-one households invited to Leyla's, thirty were represented in person by eight o'clock. The last to come was Lovely Avşin, who, after feeding and bathing Medine, appeared at the stroke of 8:30. Turned upon her were the evil eyes of malicious matrons, the admiring eyes of gaggles of girls, the wide eyes of children mesmerized by this sighting of a real *peri*, and the staring eyes of men who, awaiting dinner up on the rooftop, away from their wives, sighed loudly and hungrily. A gold coin gleams no less brightly when owned by another.

On the rooftop, spread over the shaken out and sponged down *kilim* carpets, were the daisies and hyacinths, the checks and stripes of the fringed tablecloths on either side of which the men would enjoy their dinner and cigarettes in the open air amid sweeping views. Shoes were still being removed and placed in an out-of-the-way corner, as newcomers climbed the ladder one rung and one man at a time. Our Village was awash in the soft incandescence of the setting sun, a sight some writers are inclined to describe in terms pastoral or romantic, but the men on the rooftop were having none of it. Completely unremarked upon went this glimpse of the divine being presented by nature on a silver platter, so deep were these men in their talk of animals and fields, of guard duty, and of the daughters they hoped to marry off someday soon – with the exception, of course, of Halil.

Standing atop the leaning ladder to pass on the plates being handed up by Leyla's brother, İsmail, Halil spent the few seconds between plates marveling at a world cruel yet wondrous, his heart overflowing, his stomach churning in awe, his mind adrift at sea. Without waiting for permission to caress Maral, the sun was setting her aglow, tinting her yellow and orange, bathing her golden eyes, her dimple sweeter than honey and her coiling black hair, red. In a few years, shortly after an engagement like this one, the long-awaited moment would come and he would finally take Maral in his arms. The third plate shattered, Uncle Cemal cursed, and Halil snapped out of it. There was still extra meat and rice, true, but only so much food and crockery, and besides, he was holding things up. The men were hungry and waiting. His head was splitting again; that must be why the plate gripped so tightly slipped from his hands, as though it had morphed into a sentient being, lost its balance and either leapt or been pulled to death by gravity. Tall Halil, who had barely survived the childhood meningitis completely forgotten a mere year afterward, who admittedly had an overactive imagination that made it difficult to concentrate, and who had been marked for life as 'clumsy,' for no reason at all, was relieved of his duties. Stepping in as his replacement was Yusuf, the brother a year his senior, but night to his day. Yusuf was his father's son: confident, hard, gutsy; and dripping with disdain for his younger sibling. Nobody tolerates either lean meat or greasy *tirit*.

Halil's softly spoken: 'Brother, my head's hurting something terrible, and I think there's a bug in my right eye, would you mind having a look at it?' was met with, 'You little pussy, what kind of man fusses over a headache, next thing you know you'll be bitching about bleeding every month.'

The elder brother's manly mockery sent the grown men on the rooftop into roars of laughter as the younger brother was elbowed aside.

BİLAL

According to the people of Our Village, seventy-eight-year-old Adar, the grandfather of Bilal, tended to swoop in on troubled waters and was still strong enough to knock down a man half his age. When his brother, Fatma's late father, Bozo, died in his sleep a decade earlier, Adar pounced, pronouncing himself patriarch of the entire clan. His two elder brothers, ground down by their years of dealings with police and army, had neither the guts nor the desire to object. Adar's fist hit the groom-to-be in the arm, bringing him down from the clouds, and a quick jerk of the old man's chin told him it was time. Bilal went over to his father, Çeto, who was himself deep in conversation with Leyla's father, Çetin, to say that they were ready for the rings.

With apologies and greetings, Adar, Çeto, Bilal and Cemal headed for the wooden ladder somewhere beyond the milling crowd of their extended family members; mostly on the maternal side. Their bellies had been satisfied by healthy helpings of meat and rice from heaped platters, followed by four or five pieces of baklava each. The men on the roof were puffing away amid smoke swirling and dispersing against a backdrop of mostly barren lands, now in darkness. Lower City twinkled brightly somewhere in the dim glow of a half-hearted moon. Like the inner workings of a tick-tocking heirloom watch, the women moved in precision and perfect timing as they collected the empty baklava trays, rinsed them, and prepared the portions from the feast which would be assigned to the ravenous children once the ring ceremony was done. And as for the women, staving off hunger pangs was a skill honed over centuries.

Entering the room reserved for women were four men, three of them family elders. Leading the way was the grandfather of the future groom, then the fathers of the happy couple and, finally, Bilal. Leyla approached the men standing in the middle of the room. Dressed in the customary red gown, the bride-to-be was more striking than ever. The gown featured a collar round the throat and a short train, with a belt of the same cloth encircling her waist twice. Daisies white and yellow stood in tight formation, perfectly spaced, seven on each side, in two columns waist to hem. Larger daisies graced the outer sleeves, three each, and in less than an hour they, too, would be red.

Amid warnings, pinches and slaps for the children, silence soon fell. Adar blessed the young couple, wishing them a home bountiful and bounteous, lives long and prosperous, and children healthy and many, before he called for unity, solidarity and brotherhood for the clan. He then recited the all-purpose verse: 'Allah! There is no god but He - the Living, the Self-subsisting, Eternal. No slumber can seize Him nor Sleep. His are all things in the heavens and on earth...'

Leyla's delicate nose lifted as though in pursuit of a scent alluring and elusive. Bilal's eyes black as the night shone as though from a full moon within. The prayer ended, cupped hands were turned heavenward and pairs of hands ritually washed the faces of bowed heads. Adar's big-boned hands then slipped rings onto the waiting fingers of two left hands, the first one Bilal's, the second one Leyla's. 'Congratulations! May it be auspicious,' he pronounced. Men clapped each other on the back; women hugged and held back tears. Love matches are a rare source of cheer in these parts.

Bilal's fingers reached for the end of his fine mustache, and twisted. Leyla suppressed a smile; such a boy, still, and on this day of days. Maral noticed, too, and her dimple smiled on behalf of her big sister. But Maral's stomach was a drum. That thumping would not go away. Her heart and her belly were not her own, no matter how hard she tried to control them. She went and hugged her mother again. Capable, astute, caring Fatma threw her arms around her daughter and shared what she assumed were tears of joy.

Ten minutes after the ceremony began it was over, with the men back on the rooftop. Bilal now gone, Leyla caressed the ring on her finger. The women let out a collective sigh of relief; on this day, at least, their worries and work were largely done. It was nearly two hours past sunset, and time for the men to perform their final prayer of the day. The women could now sit back and eat in peace.

Adar, who had bounded to the roof ahead of the others, paused and thrust forth his head, a wolf on the scent. Eagle eyes under bushy brows scanned the surrounding area.

'Anything wrong?' asked the groom-to-be, before he was silenced by a wave of Çeto's hand.

'A sandstorm is coming,' said the patriarch, 'we need to move quickly.'

Later, much was said about that approaching storm. Those not in attendance remembered a clear night. Some mentioned a light wind coming from Other Village, carrying, perhaps, a little fine sand, but falling far short of what would normally be called a storm. An older man seemed to remember something kicking up in the daytime and lasting all night. A farmer with sun-baked skin as furrowed as his fields insisted that was untrue: 'Sandstorms are for deserts; we have dust storms here.'

'It comes to the same thing,' said someone else, at which the farmer snapped: 'You're a big know-it-all, just because you finished primary school.'

A middle-aged woman said, 'A fog dropped on Our Village, thick as lentil soup, and a dust cloud shut out the sky.'

A young man said, 'Whatever it was, dust or sand, I wouldn't call it a storm, but I was walking to my uncle's place to have some tea and couldn't see more than ten meters in front of me, that much I remember, perfectly clearly.'

A young girl said, 'Whatever you call it, I was going to drop off bread at my mother's brother's house and a whirlwind or something grabbed me and threw me twenty meters through the air before I hit the ground, and look, you can still see the mark.' She hitched up her skirt to show a policeman the bruise on the calf of her left leg.

Several years later, as ten men awaited a final decision on their fates, the public prosecutor would repeatedly return to the same question. The ten men, too, would all tell conflicting tales: 'It was sand; it was dust. A light rain, no, more a drizzle, really; no wind at all, a still evening.' The prosecutor would also fail to get a thorough account of what Adar said and did in the interval between the ring ceremony and nighttime prayers. Damsel or dame, comes to the same. The focus should be on the nineties, not on dust and sand:

'Why did Adar and family pack up their things in '94, leaving behind their house in Our Village to move to Upper City? Investigate that, not weather reports!' they told the prosecutor; that is what some of the villagers later said:

'Who killed six people that day back in '94, and why? It was just too easy to pin murder on the guerillas, and why would no one take the time for a proper investigation?' they later said. 'Were the killers and killed not from the same family back then, too? Did the last hold-outs not become guards after that day, joining all the other village men? So much needs saying, but nobody can say it,' they said.

Some claimed that of the six dead bodies that day, three were women, three men. No, two males and four females, and of those four, two were children. One of the six was the grandmother of the killers, someone sadly added. 'Check to see who wanted village guards in the village, and who didn't,' they said.

'The state turns a blind eye to the shamelessness and thievery of the guards grabbing girls and women, land and property whenever they want, raping and killing with no accountability, and then that same state comes round when it suits them to break bread with the clans, and the state is still as innocent and white as a spoon pulled out of boiling milk, because those ignorant villagers are to blame for everything, oh, is that it?' they questioned.

An Upper City greybeard with two teeth in his head brought up the oil pipelines passing through the perpetrators' property. According to him, the killers filed suit against the state-owned company transporting oil, claiming damages for a supposed crude oil spill that happened on their land. In reality, they had used a welding tool to open a hole and then tapped into the pipeline, selling tanker truck after tanker truck of crude. The company countersued, of course.

'Not only were they killers, they were sneaky, too,' the two-toothed man added.

The company pointed out that village guards were on duty where the crude was stolen, so it must have been an inside job.

'Back then, the killer and the killers got along fine,' the old man continued. 'They were stealing together. They must have squabbled over the spoils. There are four other cases pending against those crude oil thieves, did you know that, mister newsman?' someone else told the reporter peppering mourners with questions just three days after the incident. 'Ask how those old lawsuits ended, ask why nobody stopped the stealing, ask who's protecting these guys, and why?' they said.

The company requested certification of the title deeds to confirm ownership of the land in question. But the killers never came through, because the land belonged not to them, but to those who moved away in the '80s and '90s, a villager explained. 'Who else is profiting from the crude oil racket? Are they in Lower City, or in the Red City? It would be impossible for all that money to slosh around without the military. Once the cart's overturned, everyone claims to know a less bumpy road.'

HALİL

During *namaz* in the open air, too, there was no relief for his throbbing head; his timing was off as he bent over, hands on his knees, and as he prostrated himself on his prayer rug; and the verses memorized as a child were eluding him. He kept blinking his eyes in search of a cure. Halil was worn out. The pain, the heat, the walk to Other Village: everything since morning had sapped his strength. If only *namaz* would finish so he could get home and into bed. Tomorrow was a new day, and no way would this damn pain last into the next day! Unable to go on, and willing to risk the fury of his father and the committing of a sin, he got up and sank back down in a corner of the rooftop. He took his head between his hands, rocking it back and forth. He felt like plucking out his right eye, that's how much it hurt. He began watching his worshiping relatives, who were still going through the ritual motions and would never dare to stop midway as they swayed, rose and fell, clasped their hands over their chests and mouthed the sacred words. There were so many men, far more than the thirty or thirty-five expected by Aunt Fatma ; there must have been around sixty-five, at least. He looked around. The village was blurred. The wind had died down. Out of the corner of his eye he caught a glimpse of someone on Zozan's roof. His head swiveled and he saw one, or was it two, shadowy figures on Aunt Nasibe's roof. There was someone on Village Headman Ömer's rooftop, too, holding a rifle. Information sometimes led to a beefed-up security presence in the village, but the sight of all these guards was making him uneasy. They hadn't been there before *namaz*, he was sure of that, despite the pain and grogginess. A great weight pressed down on him; the ox that always sat on his chest while passing the cemetery. He took deep breaths. He recited a prayer. He was about to look over at Zozan's rooftop again when his eyes filled with sand. The storm Grandpa Adar warned about had arrived. The prayers continued, their performance unaltered in any way, same as always. The angels must be protecting their eyes from all this sand, Halil whispered, bowing his head.

SALİH

In the middle of Namaz, heart-of-jelly-coated-in-tin Osman, mustache-of-sweatbeads-not-bristle Ismail and Psycho-Ramazan all came up onto the rooftop. The worshippers' weapons were at their sides, as always in these parts. The newcomers surprised no one. They were not the first men to show up late to an engagement or wedding; guard duty comes with unpredictable hours. Nearly done with his prayers, Adar glanced over at rotten-egg Osman and nodded, but dirty-dog Osman returned the greeting with gunfire. Straight after that, Ramazan grabbed his Kalashnikov. Fifteen-year-old İsmail was on look-out duty at the top of the ladder. At the opposite end of the rooftop, Halil froze for a short moment. Concealed, he hoped, by the clouds of dust and smoke, he jumped for Nasibe's roof. From there, he would go through into the courtyard to warn the women.

Scarecrow Salih, İdris and Mahmut made for the women's room. Gunshots are a part of life in this village; some of the women thought a skirmish had broken out over by the police station; others assumed that with Namaz now over the men were firing celebratory shots into the air. Nobody found anything strange. Breaking news would report that the assailants were masked. Some said it was an honest mistake; some said it was sensationalism; some said it was done deliberately to frame the guerrillas. That last one was the only disproved accusation amid all the contradictory claims. The triggermen were not masked; they strolled right in because they were family. If in the same house lives the mysterious thief, then through the chimney goes the missing ox. Afterwards, 'May God smite whoever armed those killers in the first place,' was the black-blessing said by some. 'Never hang liver on a cat's neck,' they said.

At the door to the women's room Salih stopped shifting from foot to foot when he saw his big brother come down from the rooftop, the job done, and to Osman's blazing eyes and bloody hands he said, 'Wh-what about the women?'

'Kill them,' said his big brother.

MARAL

When three armed men burst into the women's room, Maral knew she would never get out alive, just as she knew that drumming sensation in her stomach. Her little brother Nisar was gobbling down a chunk of meat and she covered his body with hers without thinking. Out of nowhere, in came what seemed an army of men; then bullets everywhere, overhead, on all sides, women yelling, trying to protect their babies, and their girls, and their boys, screaming, bleating lambs falling to the wolves. She held her breath, clapped a hand over Nisar's mouth, and kept an arm wrapped tight around him. Cushions wiped down and dried in the sun; white lace edged with embroidered hearts, butterflies and five-leaf clovers; *kilims* tumbled onto by toddlers; tablecloths yellow and purple, patterned with branches and leaves, roses and tulips – all were drenched in the blood of women, girls, boys, babies nursing and those still in the womb.

It ended as quickly as it began. Or so it seemed to Maral. Later, it would emerge that the triggermen from the roof rained down death for a full twenty minutes. She waited until the noise stopped. She heard a truck. Snapped orders. Then single-shot firearms, so different from the staccato in the room (here, even children know a rifle from a shotgun, a semi- from a fully automatic). To the moaning of women and children, Maral took her hand off her brother's mouth. She shook him; 'Get up gold eyes'. Nisar did not move. She tried to pick him up and saw blood on her own chest. At first she thought she had been shot, and–but only later would she realize this–she had, but in the stomach, not the chest. The blood gushing from her little brother's neck was what was feeding the growing stain across her breast. Nisar's soul was gone, leaving a body behind, and this time she clapped both hands over her own mouth to keep from howling. Thinking that the truck might have left some men behind to finish the job, Maral took careful, slow steps, and she was right there too, but that she would never know.

There were three survivors–Halil, a two-year-old boy and an eighteen-year-old girl, the latter the sole witness permitted to take the stand in court, who swore in her deposition that the attackers strafed the room with Kalashnikovs before firing at close range into the heads of anyone still breathing. By the time Maral picked her way through the bodies of women, girls, little boys, babies born and unborn, the last of the triggermen had disappeared back into the darkness.

Trailing red droplets and smears, Maral stepped through the splintered front door. She passed the rack of shoes and slippers, big and small, in all colours but now all red. She saw a few men prone in the courtyard, where they must have fallen from the roof. The courtyard door was open all the way; someone, a tall man most likely shot in the back while fleeing, was draped over the low door like a giant evil-eye amulet. Her face a sheet of parchment from loss of blood, trembling at the hell in which she found herself, Maral decided to go back into the house, thinking only of her mother, her big sister Leyla, her ten-year-old sister Helin, her seven-year-old brother Evin and her five-year-old brother Mehmet. First, she peered up onto the rooftop, where İsmail, grown to a man of eight-years-old, had had dinner with his father. But there was not a sound, as though, their prayers done, the men had plunged into a reverent silence.

Swaying unsteadily as she passed through the doorway, Maral stopped when her foot caught on something. She looked down: a small body. She stumbled again; the body's mother, probably, their arms reaching for each other. She recognized Helin's eyeglasses outside the women's room. A birthday present from one month earlier; those pink frames and those thick lenses for her nearsighted little sister. The glasses she never took off, the ones she insisted on wearing to bed she loved them so. Another step, a daisy-covered gown, and she recognized her sister Leyla laying there. She went into the room, to a strange smell, sharp and foul; the smell of death, she realised. A lake of blood. She recognized her mother from the yellow and red Shahmarans embroidered on her blue scarf; she was shielding Mehmet still. She shook her mother, then her brother; but to no avail. Slowly she looked around; was anyone still alive? A crying baby, a whimpering boy, a moaning woman or two. Among so many dead, she was trying to find the mouths of bodies able to make sounds when, with no more blood to lose, she fell onto a dead body. With one last effort, she opened her eyes and looked: Evin. With her last breath she put her arm around the brother who had breathed his last long ago. Seen from a distance, they were locked in an embrace.

The children who had been left at home, sixty of them in all, now orphans aged one through to twenty, would for many weeks cling to the tombstones of their mothers, fathers, sisters, brothers and relatives. The few remaining grown-ups would coax them to come home. The social workers specialized in trauma coming first from Upper City, then, a day or two later, from the Capital and Straits City, would advise that the children be allowed to mourn in their own way, and so they were left to cry alone, together, in the graveyard, day and night, while their elders keened and wailed for the dead in a corner.

Essentially, the perpetrators had killed their own uncles, aunts and wet nurses, along with all of their children and babies. That is what the few surviving adults said as they tried to care for the army of orphans.

'They attempted to kill all of their maternal relatives so they could take over the entire village,' they said. 'They killed everyone so there would be no witnesses,' they said.

Hoping to head off a blood feud, the imams arriving from Upper City stressed, over and over, that religion proscribes the taking of another's life, but that did not stop two men and four boys from taking an oath of vengeance. After the next general election, or the one after that, the usual general amnesty would be announced and the killers released, at which the two men and four boys would hunt them down:

'We know who the killers are, so we'll make our move when the time is ripe,' they were saying in the coffeehouse, someone said. There was no way to know if this was true. Everyone's pot was boiling with the lid on.

When the reporters were chased out of Our Village, they tracked down the near and distant relatives scattered in Town, Lower City, Upper City, Bursa, İzmir, and Mersin for a statement.

'Clan relations got complicated in 2006 when the land registry came to the village.' That is what a woman from Lower City would explain to a well-mannered lady reporter she had taken a shine to: 'Those who had migrated years earlier were blocked from returning to claim their land. In fact, one who did come back got beaten so badly he required medical treatment, which is something I know from the human rights office in Lower City where he filed a complaint, medical report in hand. Those families, and I'm referring to both families here, the killers and the killed, continued claiming all the lands as their own from that year onward. Two weeks before the engagement party, officials from the land registry came again, or so we heard, and that's when the old dispute boiled over because the deceased wanted to cut a deal with those who left in the '80s and '90s, and the killers wanted to claim the land rights as theirs only. Our ancestors died for this land, and now it's ours, they insisted.'

That is what the woman from Lower City said.

A consensus was not reached on the number of dead, either. Some said five women were pregnant, bringing the death toll to over fifty, if you included the fetuses. Some said that if you subtracted the three survivors from the sixty-five attendees, you got over sixty bodies. Some said that fifty attended the engagement party, not sixty, so fewer than fifty lives were lost. Some houses will never welcome a bride and no house is ever spared a death, but no heart can bear this much death; on this point, all were agreed.

And someone asked this: 'Why, when the guerrillas had decided to put down their arms until June, did this happen in May?'

'This place is like a furious volcano feeding on itself,' they said. 'It's been drowning in hot lava for centuries and out of some cold ashes your prosecutor is trying to make a case.'

HALİL

After jumping from Aunt Nasibe's rooftop to Fatty Bekir's, Halil went down to the street and wound round the back of Aunt Leyla's house to get to the room with the women, where he intended to help Maral, his mother, his sister Elif and all of his aunts. But it did not work out that way. He fell short, ending up sprawled on the ground in front of Nasibe's house. A meter at most separated the two rooftops; what should have been an effortless leap for those long legs of his turned out not to be. He missed. His right foot licked the corner of the roof, several meters off target, off in another dimension, it seemed.

The mist made it impossible to see; the pain made it impossible to get up; in the air was something beyond the dust and the sand, a poison that passed in through his nose and penetrated his chest with each breath. To protect himself from the bullets roaring overhead like dogfighting F16s, he tried, and failed, to curl up into a ball. His right leg was not his own. He reached for it, struggled to lift his head and have a look, and what he saw was a foot twisted backward, just like Satan Emir's.

Footsteps; someone approaching. Burying his face in the dirt road, he played dead. Men trying to make out what was ten meters ahead did not notice Halil two meters away, or they would have prodded him with a rifle butt and finished him off with a bullet to the head, just like the women and children. Salih would curse the moment in front of the door when he asked his big brother that fateful question; though again, only later. Osman was a cards-close-to-the-chest, no-tracks-in-the-snow kind of guy. Had this been his plan all along? Or had he acted in the moment? After the incident, Salih would say to the prosecutor: 'Kill them, my big brother said, so I did. Now I regret it.'

Half-dead, half-alive Halil was bloodied all along his right side, eye to hand, hip to toenail. One bullet had grazed his eye, the other had hit his hip bone. Half-conscious, half-unconscious, he gazed at the bullet-punctured tires near his head. This cannot be, he thought; did they really vow to destroy every single person, animal and thing in the village? And yet they did; this was true, for not a living soul was to be left behind in Our Village. To stop anyone from escaping, they shot at every car, tractor and truck they saw. The attackers knew Our Village like the back of their hand and under cover of dust and mist had easily fled the scene; that is what the papers would say. Because the ambulances arrived only after two hours, as did the military police, the handful of villagers who had come running from their homes to Leyla's wanted to drive the wounded to the Lower City hospital, but to no avail: all life had seeped out of the holes in the tyres of their vehicles, too.

And so the few survivors that could have been saved, were not. Later, the news reports stated that the guards posted on the rooftop had shot anyone attempting to flee; this was true. But most were in no state to get to their feet, let alone attempt to run away.

The minutes of playing dead passed for Halil. Or perhaps the hours. His memory enjoyed playing tricks on him at the best of times. It was all a muddle. His right eye hurt even worse than during the day, so badly that he felt like plucking it out. He could smell gunpowder, blood, dust. The booms and cracks of gunfire gave way to the shouts of people, one to another. And then there was the sobbing. Sobs in all ages, tones and timbres. Willing himself to get to his feet, Halil hauled himself up, his hands on the car, steadying. He began hobbling to Maral's house, his right foot dragging, the sum of his sufferings made flesh in the form of a foot turned tail trailing behind him. Two people were running toward him, but they were impossible to make out. Ah, Jinn-Jinxed Raziye's sisters, two of them; and so like each other! Halil held his hand over his right eye to staunch the bleeding, took it back off, and looked again: Now there was only one girl. Keeping his right eye closed did nothing for the pain, but it did help him to see more clearly. And when he managed to take a step, he felt for the first time since morning as though he was on solid ground, bad foot or not. When Jinn-Jinxed Raziye's sister Esma reached out her arm he knew where it was, and grabbed it tight. So tightly Esma fell to the ground, taking him with her.

Halil could not remember how long he lay there, when he was rescued or how he ended up in a hospital in Lower City. Although the prosecutor listened to him carefully, his reliability as a witness would be contested and his testimony barred from the official record due to a memory disruption condition linked to childhood meningitis. When he woke up in hospital in a cast, his head bandaged, it was not his father and mother, his brothers and sisters, or even Chunky he asked about; it was golden eyed Maral.

And so, this is what happened on the night Our Village was illuminated by a half-hearted moon and an unlucky wind swept in. The night black clouds concealed the skies, and a sandstorm, dust and mist descended out of nowhere; that ill-fated night a red devil rode the fog roughshod over the streets and ten meters was too far to see. But then again, things may have happened differently.... I am, after all, a wandering eye, a cockeye, a cross-eye. I was damaged the morning Chunky sent Halil flying. I've been somewhat adrift ever since. In places I may have said too little and in places too much. Believe what you will.

To Abidin, Filiz, Heja and Dr. Okan,
with gratitude and friendship.

* * *

AFTERWORD

It was 2012. A friend, the writer and editor Yiğit Değer Bengi, told me he was compiling an anthology of short stories themed '*against the darkness*'. The anthology never happened, but the original draft of *Engagement* was born. The story was inspired by a true-life event horrific beyond even the darkest act of imagination.

When I read the news account of what had transpired in the village of Bilge on the 4th of May, 2009, I was unable to process it: 44 people mown down by relatives bearing the same surname. Yes, human beings are capable of atrocities worse than the demons depicted in their holy books. That much I knew. But to open fire on all those people, children, pregnant women…?

After my family moved to the Netherlands in 2017, *Engagement* was relegated to a file on my desk. The first and final drafts featured a mysterious narrator revealed only at the end. But the original plot hinged on two main characters: the sister of the girl getting engaged that night and the brother of the ringleader, who reportedly killed himself in prison. It was my interest in the theme of 'otherness' that caused Halil, the protagonist of *Engagement,* to make a surprise appearance in later versions. His very existence was too 'Kurdish' for the authorities, his beautifully enunciated Turkish was too much for the locals, and his overall stylishness and gentleness was too 'effeminate' for the patriarchy.

A Reuters article dated May 5, 2009, provided a solid analysis: *Blood feuds and gun violence plague Turkey's southeast.* Turkish news accounts, however, were all riddled with inconsistent and missing information, from the number of assailants to whether or not they were masked. Honor killing or clash of competing interests? When exactly did the military police and ambulances arrive on the scene, and why were they so late? What were the weather conditions that day?

Other than through a visit to the area, in-person interviews, and contradictory articles, I was unable to unearth many hard facts. Reporting by human rights associations and academics proved to be invaluable to my research. This dearth of information made me even more determined not to allow the massacre to be forgotten; we owed at least this much to the lives extinguished that day. And as an author, I was best placed to create a fictionalized account of that day's events.

On September 10, 2021, during an interview with Aynur Kulak for online culture and arts magazine *Artfulliving.com.tr*, I asked: From what I gather in news accounts, over 60 children were orphaned that night; so where are they? Well, one of them found me after the book was published.

Zeynep and I spoke for over two hours on the phone. We later met in person and over time we became friends. I am in awe of her. That night, she lost parents and three of her siblings. When I asked her where she was living, she replied, 'I haven't got a fixed home.' Despite having to stay at various dormitories and with friends, Zeynep managed to graduate from university with a high GPA while holding down a job at a prestigious firm as she aspired to complete her master's degree abroad. Every time I think about the strength and humanity of this 23-year-old woman who is still battling daily to transform her pain and grief into self-realization, and whose dream it is to one day provide financial and moral support to the people of troubled regions wherever they are, I get tears in my eyes. When I asked her what I could do, Zeynep said, 'It is enough that you help give us a voice, raise awareness and remember that we still exist.'

As far as we know, the killers are currently in prison. Some of their relatives, who had migrated for safety reasons, have returned to the village. What Reuters wrote about that region some 15 years ago is equally valid today: *Experts say the problem, which is more acute in the Kurdish southeast, is aggravated by unequal land distribution, power struggles in a feudal-style clan system and a decision by the government to set up well-armed village militias against Kurdish rebels.*

Compounding this grim reality of life for the dozens of children and babies orphaned that day is the fact that they still face property disputes with their grasping relatives over land belonging to their dead parents, suffer economic hardships, stay in orphanages, and in some cases are left with no choice but to return in an arranged marriage to the village where their parents were murdered.

As for the rest of us, we can only continue to hope for change. And to believe in the power of love and friendship.

Çiler İlhan

A short story writer and novelist, İlhan is the author of four books: **Hayattayız Madem** (Everest Yayınları, 2023); **Engagement** (Nişan Evi, Everest, 2021); *Exile* (Sürgün, Everest Publications, 2010) winner of the **2011 European Union Prize for Literature,** published in over 20 countries, and *Chamber of Dream Merchants* (Rüya Tacirleri Odası, Artemis, 2006). Her short stories have been published in numerous literary magazines, while her essays, book reviews and travel writings have appeared in numerous magazine and newspaper supplements. Çiler İlhan studied International Relations and Political Science at Boğaziçi University in Türkiye, and Hotel Management at the Glion Hotel School in Switzerland. She has worked in hotel management, marketing/communications, and publishing (as an editor/writer). She's a member of Turkish and Dutch PEN. Born and raised in Türkiye, she currently lives in the Netherlands.

Kenneth Dakan

Born in Salt Lake City, Utah, Kenneth Dakan lives in Istanbul, where his focus is on literary translation from Turkish to English. Among the works of fiction and nonfiction he has translated are Perihan Magden's *Escape*, Ayse Kulin's *Farewell: A Mansion in Occupied Istanbul* and *Love in Exile*, Ece Temelkuran's *Deep Mountain*, Birgül Oğuz's **Hah!** (co-translation), Murat Somer's *Hop-Çiki-Yaya* murder mystery series and Buket Uzuner's **I am Istanbul**

Engagement
Translated from the Turkish by Kenneth Dakan

First published in English in 2024 by Istros Books
London, United Kingdom www.istrosbooks.com

Copyright ©Çiler Ilhan, 2024
First published in Turkish as *Nişan Evi*, Everest, 2021

Translation © Kenneth Dakan

ISBN: 978-1-912545-39-1
The publishers would like to express their thanks for the financial support that made the publication of this book possible:

Supported using public funding by
**ARTS COUNCIL
ENGLAND**

Milton Keynes UK
Ingram Content Group UK Ltd.
UKHW021819010524
442042UK00004B/77

9 781912 545391